Start Reading
AND WRITING

Tiddalik the Frog

Anne Faundez

Long ago, in the Dreamtime, a huge red frog roamed the earth. His name was Tiddalik. Tiddalik was so large that his back touched the sky. He was so wide that he filled the space between two mountain ranges. When he moved, the ground trembled and his feet made holes as big as valleys.

One day, he woke up from a very bad sleep. He was VERY, VERY grumpy! He was also VERY, VERY thirsty!

"Water! Water!" he bellowed.
His words made the clouds
crackle with thunder.

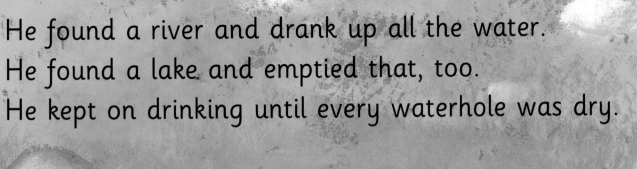

He found a river and drank up all the water.
He found a lake and emptied that, too.
He kept on drinking until every waterhole was dry.

Tiddalik was now bulging with water and ready to burst.

He was too uncomfortable to move. He shut his eyes and fell into a long, deep sleep.

The days went by.

Tiddalik slept.

8

There was no sign
of rain in the skies.

The sun scorched
the earth. The
grasses withered
and the trees lost
their leaves.

The beautiful green
earth became hard
and cracked.

Kangaroo, Kookaburra and Platypus were anxious. They had watched Tiddalik drinking up all the water. Now their land was turning to dust.

"The earth is so cracked that I can't hop around anymore," grumbled Kangaroo.

"There's nowhere for me to swim," moaned Platypus.

"Tiddalik MUST return our water!" said Kookaburra.

But the animals were scared to talk to Tiddalik. He was still so grumpy!

"I know," said Kookaburra. "Let's make him laugh. Then he'll spill out the water."

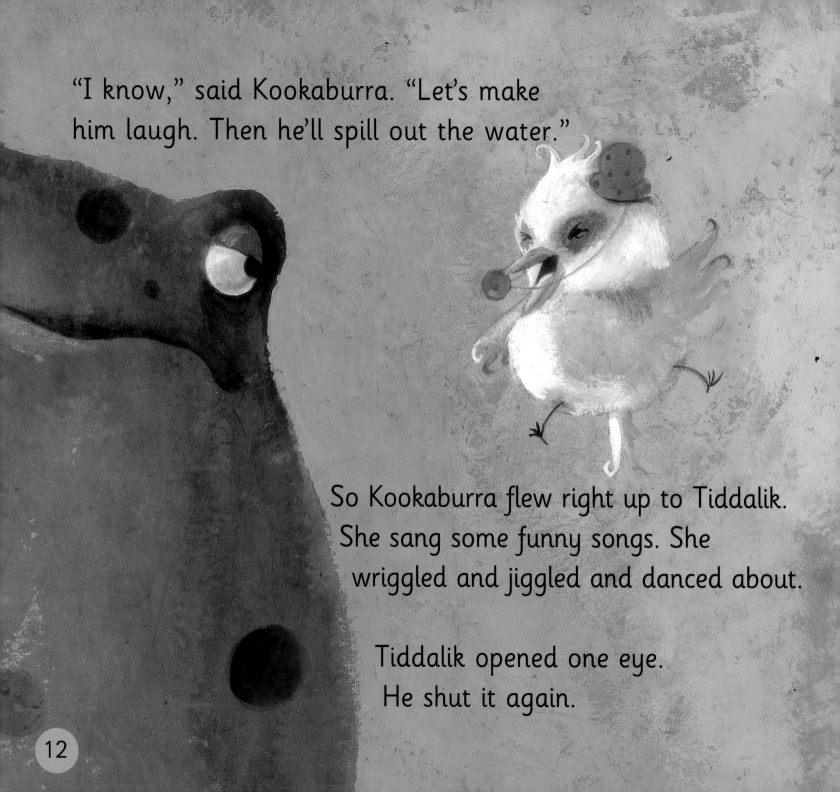

So Kookaburra flew right up to Tiddalik. She sang some funny songs. She wriggled and jiggled and danced about.

Tiddalik opened one eye. He shut it again.

Platypus went up to Tiddalik. She told a few jokes and then she flipped and flopped and shuffled about.

Tiddalik opened the other eye.
He shut it again.

13

Next, it was Kangaroo's turn.
He loved to show off.
He twirled and whirled,
and thumped and
bumped his tail around.

Tiddalik opened both eyes.
He shut them again.
He was still bored.

14

Just then, Little Eel came rushing towards the animals.

"Let me make Tiddalik laugh!" he cried.

He raced towards Tiddalik, turning somersaults all the way.

15

Little Eel landed on Tiddalik's bulging stomach.
He scrambled to get himself upright.
He teetered and tottered and then stood,
looking up at the gigantic frog.

Tiddalik opened his eyes. He was
so astonished to see Little Eel,
all shivering and shaking,
sitting right on his belly.

17

Tiddalik made a rumbling noise.
He chuckled — and a trickle of water
dribbled from his mouth.

He chuckled a bit more.

18

Soon, he was rumbling with laughter.
Water spilled from his mouth and ran down his sides.
Tiddalik couldn't stop laughing at the sight of
Little Eel sitting on his belly.
As he laughed, he felt less grumpy.

Soon, the land was awash with water.
The grasses began to grow again, and tiny leaves
began to cover the bare branches of the trees.

And do you know what? To this day, Tiddalik
has never again emptied the land of water.
Why?

Well, Little Eel knows just what to do now
when Tiddalik gets grumpy ... and thirsty!

What do you think?

How did Kookaburra
try to make
Tiddalik laugh?

Who finally
made Tiddalik
laugh?

How did Tiddalik feel when he woke up from a very bad sleep?

Can you remember the names of these animals?

Carers' and teachers' notes

- Tell your child that this story is a myth, and that a myth is a type of traditional story that sets out to explain something about the world.
- Explain that this story is an Australian Aboriginal myth, set in the Dreamtime, which was a time before people existed, when the world was new.
- More specifically, tell your child that the story is a creation myth, and sets out to explain how drought came about – and was ended.
- Talk about the characters and explain that these animals come from, and live in, Australia.
- Help your child to use a reference book to look up entries for 'Kangaroo', 'Kookaburra' and 'Platypus'.
- Look at the pictures in the book. Point out that the characters are illustrated in the same colours as the landscape. This is because the landscape is crucial to the story.
- Read the story aloud, using a different voice for each animal character.

- Look at the way dialogue is presented in the story. Dialogue is set within speech marks (inverted commas), while each character's speech is set out on a new line.
- Find the words in the story that express how the characters speak, for example, 'bellowed', 'grumbled', 'moaned' and 'cried'. Have fun practising the characters' speeches in the tones suggested by these words.
- Point out the use of alliteration, for example, 'flipped and flopped' and 'shivering and shaking'. Have fun making up some more alliterative phrases.
- Can your child suggest why the word 'VERY' on page 5 is written in capital letters? (For emphasis.) Show your child how to read the sentence, with the stress on the word 'VERY'.
- Talk about your child's favourite character. Encourage him/her to paint a picture of this favourite character, set within the landscape.